Angel Friends
Let Your Smile Shine

by Tara Williams
Illustrations by Aniena Simone

SR
Stillwater
River

Visit our website at **www.StillwaterPress.com** for more information.
First Stillwater River Publications Edition

ISBN-10: 1-946-30023-3
ISBN-13: 978-1-9463002-3-2

1 2 3 4 5 6 7 8 9 10
Written by Tara Williams
Illustrated by Aniena Simone
Cover Design by Dawn M. Porter
Published by Stillwater River Publications, Glocester, RI, USA.

*The views and opinions expressed in this book are solely those of the author
and do not necessarily reflect the views and opinions of the publisher.*

Dedication

To my sweet Aria – Let your smile shine!

"The first day of school, the first day of school! Oh yes, I'm ready for the first day of school!" India sang.

"Well I'm a little nervous for our first day," whispered Aria. "We will have a new teacher, new friends, and lots of homework."

Just then Julia, India's angel friend gently flew by.

"Oh girls, there is nothing to worry about." Then she began to sing. "Just take a deep breath and think happy thoughts. Your smiles will light up the room. Have no fear and remember that your angel friends are always near!"

"Good luck and have fun!"

"Good morning, classity class!" said a sweet voice. "I am your teacher, Mrs. Asher. We are going to start learning about each other by writing about your summer vacation."

The children began raising and waving their hands. Mrs. Asher smiled and said, "Oh, I love your excitement. I can't wait to hear about everyone's summer."

All the children got to work quickly.

"Time's up," said Mrs. Asher. "Tommy, would you like to go first?" Tommy stood up, adjusted his glasses, and shared his story. He went to summer camp, caught frogs, and learned how to swim.

India was called. She went to the front of the class and shared her story about being on the gymnastics team. She even did a back-flip to show everyone what she learned!

Livvy was next, and she shared how she was at her grandma's all summer in a different state. She learned how to milk a cow and help out on the farm.

Then it was Aria's turn to share. She slowly got up and spoke about her summer surgery. She was born with something called a cleft lip. Sometimes it was hard for her to eat and speak. Aria had to go to the hospital to have surgery in order to fix her lip and nose. Now she had a red scar on her face. The doctors fixed it, but Aria knew she looked a little different.

The children began to raise their hands with questions for Aria.

"Were you scared?" asked Tommy.

"I was scared, but I tried to be brave."

"Did it hurt?" asked India.
"It only hurt a little bit after, but they gave me medicine and lots of freeze pops."

"How long will you have the scar for?" asked Livvy.
"I will have this scar on my face forever, but the doctor told me it would fade with time."

"You sure are a brave little girl," Mrs. Asher said.

Just then, the recess bell rang.

At recess the children decided to play hide and seek. Livvy began to count... "Ready or not here I come," Livvy shouted.

"Scargirl! Where are you?" "Oh scargirl..."

The other students looked around for Aria and felt very uncomfortable.

Aria was hiding behind a tree and she melted to the ground. She began to cry. India hurried over to hug her.

"It's okay friend. Livvy is just being mean."

"Yeah," said Tommy, "I'm different too. I'm the only one in that class that wears glasses. Even Livvy is different. She has red curly hair."

"After all," said India, "there is something different about each one of us. But we are all beautiful."

"You are amazing," said a voice from above their heads. It was Michael, Aria's angel friend.

"Sometimes when people aren't happy with themselves they tease other people. It is very unkind and not fair but one day they will learn. For now, you hold your head up high, walk away, and sing this song."

"I will smile, and I will shine.
Look at me, I'm just fine.
I won't let you bring me down.
You won't even see me frown.
I will smile, and I will shine.
Look at me, I'm just fine!"

"Come on, it's time to go in. I'll spend the rest of the day with you," said Michael reassuringly.

"**C**lassity class! Everyone get your crayons out. It's time for art," said Mrs. Asher.

"Today you will be drawing a self-portrait to hang up for parent night. When your parents come in, they will have to guess which picture is their child?

Livvy quietly leaned over to Aria. "Your mom will definitely know where your picture is ...the only one with the scarface," she said, laughing.

Aria wilted in her chair. Michael quickly flew behind Aria. "Remember Aria, many people are afraid of what is different and you are different. That is a wonderful thing. You stand out like a shining star. So shine that light for everybody to see!"

Aria sat up a little taller in her chair and began drawing a beautiful self-portrait.

Books!
Get ready, get set, READ!
Markers
coloured Pencil
computer paper
Lined
Extra No. 2 Pencils
Pens and

The clock struck three o'clock. It was time to go home. India and Aria skipped out of the school yard with Michael by their side. They were talking about how awesome their teacher was when Livvy skated by.

"Scargirl, Scargirl," Livvy yelled.

"Stop right there," India said bravely. "You are not being very nice to my friend. She is a great person with a big heart. You need to change those mean voices inside your head and choose kindness instead, or no one will want to play with you. The choice is yours."

Aria stood proudly and said, "Livvy you should try being kind. I know you will feel better about yourself."

Livvy picked up her skateboard and walked away quietly with her head down.

Aria gave India a hug, and with a gentle breeze, Michael flew away.

Aria and India began to sing the rest of the walk home.

"I will smile, and I will shine.
Look at me, I'm just fine.
I won't let you bring me down.
You won't even see me frown.
I will smile, and I will shine.
Look at me, I'm just fine!"

The next morning the girls were playing jump rope in the school yard.
One, two, three, jump with me…la la la la la la

Livvy slowly walked over to Aria. "I'm very sorry for teasing you. It wasn't nice. I promise not to tease anyone anymore! I really hope we can all be friends this year."

India and Aria looked at each other, smiled and let their light shine through. "We can!" they said at the same time giggling. "Come on. Let's play."
One, two, three, jump with me …la la la la la la la.

The End

How to handle bullies?
SMILE
Stand up for yourself
Move away/Avoid
Ignore
Let an adult know
Exhale

A READERS' THEATER PLAY

Readers' Theater is a dramatic presentation of a written work in a script form. **Readers** read from a "script" and reading parts are divided among the **readers.** No memorization, costumes, blocking or special lighting is needed. Presentations can easily be done in a K-3 classroom Scripts are held by the **readers.**

Angel Friends: Let Your Smile Shine

People in the play

ARIA

INDIA

LIVVY

MICHAEL

JULIA

TOMMY

MRS. ASHER

INDIA : THE FIRST DAY OF SCHOOL, THE FIRST DAY OF SCHOOL! OH YES, I'M READY FOR THE FIRST DAY OF SCHOOL!

ARIA: I'M A LITTLE NERVOUS FOR OUR FIRST DAY. WE WILL HAVE A NEW TEACHER, NEW FRIENDS, AND LOTS OF HOMEWORK.

INDIA: LOOK, IT'S A FEATHER. JULIA MUST BE NEAR!

(INDIA'S ANGEL FRIEND GENTLY FLEW BY.)

JULIA : HELLO, GIRLS! ARE YOU READY FOR AN AMAZING FIRST DAY OF SCHOOL? I HEAR YOU HAVE AN AWESOME TEACHER. YOU ARE SURE TO HAVE A REMARKABLE YEAR!

INDIA: ARIA IS A LITTLE WORRIED.

JULIA: OH GIRLS, THERE IS NOTHING TO WORRY ABOUT. JUST TAKE A DEEP BREATH AND THINK HAPPY THOUGHTS. YOUR SMILES WILL LIGHT UP THE

ROOM. HAVE NO FEAR AND REMEMBER THAT YOUR ANGEL FRIENDS ARE ALWAYS NEAR!

GOOD LUCK AND HAVE FUN!

☺ MRS. ASHER: GOOD MORNING, CLASSITY CLASS! I AM YOUR TEACHER, MRS. ASHER. WE ARE GOING TO START LEARNING ABOUT EACH OTHER BY WRITING A STORY ABOUT WHAT YOU DID OVER SUMMER VACATION? I CAN'T WAIT TO HEAR ABOUT EVERYONE'S SUMMER.

(ALL THE CHILDREN GOT TO WORK QUICKLY)

TIME'S UP! TOMMY, WOULD YOU LIKE TO GO FIRST?

☺ TOMMY: I WENT TO SUMMER CAMP. I CAUGHT FROGS AND LEARNED HOW TO SWIM. IT WAS SO COOL!

MRS. ASHER: VERY NICE TOMMY. INDIA YOU ARE NEXT.

INDIA: I WAS ON THE GYMNASTICS TEAM THIS SUMMER. I LEARNED HOW TO DO A BACK FLIP!

MRS. ASHER: AWESOME INDIA! LIVVY IT'S YOUR TURN.

LIVYY: I WENT TO MY GRANDMA'S ALL SUMMER. I LEARNED HOW TO MILK A COW AND I HELPED ON THE FARM.

MRS. ASHER: GREAT LIVVY. ARIA YOU CAN COME UP NEXT.

(ARIA SLOWLY GETS UP TO SPEAK, WITH HER HEAD DOWN.)

ARIA: I HAD TO GO TO THE HOSPITAL TO HAVE A SURGERY TO FIX MY CLEFT LIP. SOMETIMES IT WAS HARD FOR ME TO EAT AND TALK SO THE DOCTOR NEEDED TO FIX IT.

TOMMY: WERE YOU SCARED?

ARIA: I WAS A SCARED, BUT I TRIED TO BE BRAVE AND THOUGHT HAPPY THOUGHTS.

INDIA: DID IT HURT?

ARIA: IT ONLY HURT A LITTLE BIT AFTER, BUT THEY GAVE ME MEDICINE AND LOTS OF FREEZE POPS TO HELP ME FEEL BETTER.

LIVVY: HOW LONG WILL YOU HAVE THE SCAR ON YOUR FACE FOR?

ARIA: I WILL HAVE THIS SCAR ON MY FACE FOREVER, BUT THE DOCTOR TOLD ME IT WOULD FADE WITH TIME.

MRS. ASHER: YOU SURE ARE A BRAVE LITTLE GIRL.

(THE RECESS BELL RINGS)

ALL STUDENTS: YES! RECESS TIME!

LIVVY: TIME FOR HIDE AND SEEK! READY OR NOT HERE I COME. SCARGIRL! WHERE ARE YOU? OH SCARGIRL…

(ARIA WAS HIDING BEHIND A TREE, CRYING)

INDIA: IT'S OKAY FRIEND, LIVVY IS JUST BEING MEAN.

TOMMY: YEAH, I'M DIFFERENT TOO. I'M THE ONLY ONE IN THAT CLASS WHO WEARS GLASSES. EVEN LIVVY IS DIFFERENT. SHE HAS RED CURLY HAIR.

INDIA: AFTER ALL, THERE IS SOMETHING DIFFERENT ABOUT EACH ONE OF US. BUT WE ARE ALL BEAUTIFUL.

MICHAEL: YOU ARE BEAUTIFUL. SOMETIMES WHEN PEOPLE AREN'T HAPPY WITH THEMSELVES THEY TEASE OTHER PEOPLE. IT IS VERY UNKIND AND NOT FAIR BUT ONE DAY THEY WILL LEARN. FOR NOW, YOU HOLD YOUR HEAD UP HIGH, WALK AWAY, AND SING THIS SONG.

> I WILL SMILE, AND I WILL SHINE. LOOK AT ME, I'M JUST FINE.
>
> I WON'T LET YOU BRING ME DOWN. YOU WON'T EVEN SEE ME FROWN.
>
> I WILL SMILE, AND I WILL SHINE. LOOK AT ME, I'M JUST FINE!

COME ON, IT'S TIME TO GO IN. I'LL SPEND THE REST OF THE DAY WITH YOU.

MRS. ASHER : CLASSITY CLASS! EVERYONE GET YOUR CRAYONS OUT. IT'S TIME FOR ART. TODAY YOU WILL BE DRAWING A SELF-PORTRAIT TO HANG UP FOR PARENT NIGHT. WHEN YOUR PARENTS COME IN, THEY WILL HAVE TO GUESS WHICH PICTURE IS THEIR CHILD. IT WILL BE SO MUCH FUN! SO TRY YOUR BEST!

LIVVY: *(WHISPERING TO ARIA)* YOUR MOM WILL DEFINITELY KNOW WHERE YOUR PICTURE IS … THE ONLY ONE WITH THE SCARFACE!

(ARIA WILTED IN HER CHAIR.)

MICHAEL: REMEMBER ARIA, MANY PEOPLE ARE AFRAID OF WHAT IS DIFFERENT AND YOU ARE DIFFERENT. YOU ARE UNIQUE! THAT IS A WONDERFUL THING. YOU, ARIA STAND OUT LIKE A SHINING STAR. SO SHINE THAT LIGHT FOR EVERYBODY TO SEE!

(ARIA SAT UP A LITTLE TALLER IN HER CHAIR)

(BELL RINGS)

ALL STUDENTS: YAY! IT'S TIME TO GO HOME!

LIVVY: SCARGIRL, SCARGIRL!

INDIA: STOP RIGHT THERE. YOU ARE NOT BEING VERY NICE TO MY FRIEND. SHE IS A GREAT PERSON WITH A BIG HEART. YOU NEED TO CHANGE THOSE MEAN VOICES INSIDE YOUR HEAD AND CHOOSE KINDNESS INSTEAD, OR NO ONE WILL WANT TO PLAY WITH YOU. THE CHOICE IS YOURS.

ARIA: YOU KNOW, LIVVY, YOU CAN SHINE YOUR LIGHT BY BEING KIND. YOU SHOULD TRY IT. I JUST KNOW YOU WILL FEEL BETTER ABOUT YOURSELF AND EVERYONE ELSE.

(LIVVY PUTS HER HEAD DOWN TO THINK)

ARIA, MICHAEL & INDIA: *(SING)* I WILL SMILE, AND I WILL SHINE. LOOK AT ME, I'M JUST FINE. I WON'T LET YOU BRING ME DOWN. YOU WON'T EVEN SEE ME FROWN. I WILL SMILE, AND I WILL SHINE. LOOK AT ME, I'M JUST FINE!

LIVVY : YOU ARE RIGHT GIRLS. I'M VERY SORRY FOR TEASING YOU. IT WASN'T NICE. I PROMISE NOT TO TEASE ANYONE ANYMORE! I REALLY HOPE WE CAN ALL BE FRIENDS THIS YEAR.

INDIA AND ARIA: OF COURSE WE CAN! COME ON. LET'S PLAY!

INDIA, ARIA, & LIVVY: ONE, TWO, THREE, PLAY WITH ME …LA LA LA LA LA LA LA!

About the Author

Tara began writing books when she became an early childhood educator. She realized books can be for both enjoyment and an amazing conversation starter with children. Many difficult topics can be addressed using a great book. Tara lives in Rhode Island with her husband, Chris and their daughter, Aria. Tara wants all children to always hold their heads up high and keep smiling.

About the Illustrator

Fourteen-year-old Aniena Simone is excited to start her freshman year at Chariho High School in Richmond, RI. In her eighth-grade school year, she was accepted into the National Junior Honor Society at Chariho Middle School. Always striving to make herself a better artist, Aniena actively practices by drawing and sketching daily, as well as taking weekly acrylic painting classes at Lionheart Studio in Richmond, RI. Additionally, she has taken classes at Wickford Art Association and has attended summer classes for 4 years at the Rhode Island School of Design. To this point, one of the most unusual classes she's taken was watercolour painting on yupo (a thin sheet of plastic), which she found to be extremely enjoyable. Her efforts have paid off, as Aniena has received many awards from entering art competitions. About this, she says "the one I am most proud of is being chosen for the 2017 Rhode Island State Duck Stamp; though I have won awards such as Best in Show at the Southern Rhode Island 4-H Fair and several awards, including Reserve Champion, for art entered at the Washington County Fair."